Clementine
and the Spring Trip

Clementine

and the Spring Trip

SARA PENNYPACKER

PICTURES BY
Marla Frazee

ⅅisney • HYPERION
Los Angeles   New York

Text copyright © 2013 by Sara Pennypacker
Illustrations copyright © 2013 by Marla Frazee

Many thanks to Bianca Ramirez for her drawings on pages 34 and 86–87.

For information address
Disney • Hyperion,
125 West End Avenue,
New York, New York 10023.

First hardcover edition, March 2013
First paperback edition, January 2014

10 9 8 7 6 5 4 3 2 1
FAC-025393-16074
Printed in China

Library of Congress Control number for the hardcover edition: 2011052991
ISBN 978-1-4847-8983-4

Visit www.DisneyBooks.com

*This one's for
Stephanie Lurie,
the captain of Team
Clementine . . .*
　　—S.P.

To Liz Garden Salad
　　—M.F.

Clementine

and the Spring Trip

Spring is a really big deal here in Boston, let me tell you. After all that snow and ice, the whole city goes a little crazy when the first warm weather shows up. So when my mother checked the thermometer on Sunday afternoon and announced it was time for our Annual Family Spring Walk Through Boston Common, I grabbed my sketchbook—I knew I'd see something interesting.

And I sure did, right away. At the "Make Way for Ducklings" sculpture in the Public Garden, where we always start our walk, I saw my friend

Margaret standing over the last brass duckling. She was wearing big rubber gloves and slopping soapy water on him with a sponge.

"Margaret!" I cried, running to her. "What are you doing?"

Although I knew: Margaret gets extra Margaretty when the weather turns nice. She runs around scrubbing everything in sight until it sparkles, even things that don't belong to her, like the elevator doors in our lobby and the parking meters on the street.

"Spring cleaning!" Margaret shouted, and somehow she made it sound like "It's my birthday!" and "Free candy for life!" rolled into one. She went back to scrubbing Quack's head.

My parents followed my little brother to the edge of the pond, and I sat down beside the ducklings.

"Your mother's letting you do this?" I wondered if maybe Margaret's mother had gone a little crazy with the great weather too. I looked around for her, because I would like to see Margaret's mother going a little crazy.

Margaret pointed over her shoulder to a bunch of kids playing catch. "My mother went out to lunch with Alan. Mitchell's in charge today. He said I could clean anything I wanted here, as long as I didn't touch his baseball stuff."

Margaret straightened up and shot a glare at her brother. From the way her fingers were twitching around the sponge, I could tell his rule was making her nuts. "Baseballs are supposed to be white, you know!" she yelled at him.

Mitchell pumped his glove in the air with a big smile, and went back to playing ball. Mitchell acts extra Mitchelly in the spring too. Not because of the weather, but because the Red Sox are back in town. According to Mitchell, the Red Sox are the greatest team in the history of the universe, and it's just a matter of time before they

ask him to play for them. He carries his new baseball bat around with him everywhere as if it's a third arm, and he's always grinning so hard, I think his cheeks will crack off.

"Never mind," I said to Margaret. "The ducks look great, at least."

She looked down at them. "They do, don't they?" she said with a proud smile. "I think Mrs. Mallard must be really happy now. Doesn't it look like she's trying to lead them to the pond? She's probably been wishing all these years she could just get her kids into the water and give them a nice bath, for heaven's sake."

I thought the story was more about her wanting to find them a home, but I didn't remind Margaret of this. Instead I held up my sketchbook and offered to do a drawing of the statue. "I'll put lots of sparkle rays on the ducklings to show how clean you got them. Maybe I'll put in a cow, too. It could be admiring the ducks."

"A cow?"

I nodded. "Farmers used to bring their cows here to the Common. I'm not even kidding about that, Margaret."

Margaret yelped and checked the bottoms of her shoes with a panicky look on her face.

"Not now," I explained. "In Ye Olden Times."

Margaret's face crumpled at the words *Ye Olden Times.* I knew what she was thinking about: our field trip to Plimoth Plantation coming up

on Thursday. She spread a dry rag over Mrs. Mallard's back and sank down with her head in her hands.

"They have dirt floors there, Clementine," she mumbled through her fingers. "We saw a video Friday. *Dirt!* The Pilgrims swept them every morning, as if that would make them less dirty! Those Ye Olden Times people were insane!"

Margaret raised her head and gave me a hopeful look. "Hey! You like getting dirty. You be my partner on the trip. If we have to touch anything that looks filthy, you do it."

"Oh, all right." I said it in a draggy voice and added a tragedy sigh, although secretly I was happy—I *do* like getting dirty. "But then you have to protect me from the eating-sounds people."

Ever since we had learned that the third and fourth graders were going to have lunch together on the trip, Margaret had been reminding me that the fourth graders didn't allow any eating sounds. Every time I asked her what they did if someone made a noise, she turned white and began to quake, as if the answer was too horrible to say out loud. Which was enough of an answer for me.

Margaret thought about it. "If you make any sounds, there's nothing I can do to save you," she warned. "But I can teach you what to pack for lunch so you can do silent eating. Deal?"

I held out my hand so Margaret could air-shake

it, the way she invented, so she wouldn't feel crawly with germs.

Then Margaret pointed at my sketchbook. "You can do the drawing now. Extra sparkle rays. No cows."

Just as I pulled out my pencils, though, my family came over.

Margaret gave my mother's belly a suspicious look and took a step backward. My mother laughed and told her, "Don't worry. Still a few months to go."

No matter how many times we tell her it won't happen, Margaret acts as if our baby could be born at any second, in a big explosion aiming right at her.

Margaret said, "Oh, phew, good," but I noticed she didn't come any closer. Even when my dad took a picture of her beside the shiny statue, she kept stealing nervous glances at my mom.

My parents took off after my brother again and waved for me to follow. "What are you so worried about anyway, Margaret?" I asked, as I collected my pencils.

"Babies wear diapers for a reason, you know, Clementine," she answered. "And I don't think they come with one on."

I didn't have a good answer for that, so I patted Mrs. Mallard's head and said good-bye.

It was a pretty good walk. I kept an eye out for cows, in case some farmer realized, *Hey, that was a good idea those historical people had. I'm going to be nice to my cows too, and let them have a stroll through the park!* Boston Common is a lot more interesting now, and I bet the cows would enjoy it even more. And so would I. Cows on swan boats, cows relaxing on benches, cows using Porta-Potties—I would really like to see those things.

I didn't, but there was a lot of other good stuff. We saw some kite fliers, and a woman on a unicycle, and about a million daffodils. Some

workmen were jackhammering up a curbstone, which made my brother so excited he looked like he was being electrocuted. Mostly, though, what we saw were things that seemed to be in a big hurry to get growing. Pink flower buds were bursting out of branches. Neon-green grass blades were zipping up through last year's tired brown stuff. And around each oak tree, dozens of little seedlings were shooting out of the acorns that had dropped in the fall.

And that reminded me: Last fall, I'd planted a couple of apple seeds behind our building. I hadn't checked them since the snow had melted.

As soon as we got home, I went out back to the brick wall I'd built to protect my tree when it grew up. The ground inside was covered with leaves, but when I carefully brushed them away, guess what I found!

A sprout! A real, live sprout with two sets of leaves!

I ran inside. "It's born! It's born, it's born, it's born!"

My dad shot a worried look at my mom, and my mom clapped her arms over her belly, as if they were both afraid that whoever was in there would hear me and decide to get itself born now too.

"Who's born?" they asked.

"Not a who," I said. "Follow me!"

I grabbed my mom's hand, and she grabbed my dad's hand, and he scooped my brother off the couch. I led the family parade outside to my brick wall and swept my arms out. "Ta-da!" I cried. "My apple tree is born!"

My family clapped as if I had just performed an amazing magic act. Which, actually, I had.

"I'm going to water it, and take care of it, and it's going to get really big," I told them. "And then we can have apples any time we want to."

I reached up and pretended to pick some fruit, and handed it out. Even Mung Bean got the joke and chomped down on his delicious pretend apple. And although my father insisted he found a worm in his, we all agreed they were the best we had ever eaten in our lives.

2

As soon as I sat down next to her on the bus Monday morning, Margaret started warning me about silent eating. "No crunching, no smacking, no snicking. No slurping, no gulping, no—"

"Wait. I don't even know what snicking is," I interrupted. "How can I figure out how *not* to do it if I don't know how to *do* it?"

"Snicking happens when you eat something sticky, like peanut butter, and it makes your tongue stick to the roof of your mouth," Margaret explained. "When you *un*stick it, that's snicking. So no peanut butter."

"Never mind," I said. "I'll just bring some yogurt."

Margaret bit her bottom lip. "I don't know, Clementine. Yogurt's tricky. It can't be the slurping kind. It has to be the biting kind."

"How about the drinking kind of yogurt?"

Margaret shuddered. "Glugging is the worst sound of all," she said. "It's even worse than slurping. I don't even want to think about what would happen to you if you glugged the drinking kind of yogurt."

She tapped her new ballerina lunch box. "Banana, string cheese, bread. This is what I bring every day for silent eating. Sometimes a cupcake. No frosting, though, of course, because of snicking."

"But you don't like bananas, Margaret. They're too mushy, remember? Plus, they have that gray part at the bottom tip you call the—"

"The mushroom. I know. I hate that." Margaret shrugged.

"And your mother doesn't think that's strange? That you don't like bananas but you ask her to give you one every day?"

"My mother packs my lunch, and then I unpack it and start over. Lately, she doesn't even notice. She's been acting weird. These days all of her sentences start with the word *Alan*. And he's always hanging around, trying to kiss her."

Alan is Margaret's mother's boyfriend. Margaret and Mitchell think Alan would be all right if it weren't for the kissing. "I bet I know what it is," I told Margaret. "Remember in *Bambi*, how in the spring all the animals went a little crazy about their boyfriend or girlfriend? I bet your mother and Alan are just twitterpated with each other. It happened to Rasheed and Maria in my class last week too."

"That's probably it," Margaret agreed. "They'll

probably go back to normal when it's summer. Anyway, it's a good thing, because now I can pack silent-eating food. Plus, I can take as many hand sanitizers as I want."

She opened her lunch box so I could see. A couple of sticks of string cheese and a banana looked as if they were napping on a mattress of hand sanitizer packets. This was a lot, even for Margaret, who uses a hand sanitizer wipe to sterilize the hand-sanitizer-wipe packet before she opens it.

"Hey, wait," I said after I'd thought about that for a minute. "How does that work?"

But Margaret had already snapped shut her ballerina lunch box and was bouncing off the bus.

When I walked into my classroom, I asked my teacher, "Yet?"

Mr. D'Matz shook his head. "Not yet." He tapped his watch. "Any minute now, though. I hope."

We have been doing this every morning for two weeks. My teacher's wife is overdue with their baby. This isn't like having a book overdue at the library, because nobody makes you pay a fine. But it's worse, because waiting is so hard. "Oh, sorry," I said, and then I hung up my jacket.

Instead of doing Quiet Journal Writing, everyone was running around, talking about Thursday this and Thursday that. This is because our school

goes a little crazy in the spring too. We take field trips, as if with all this good weather everybody wants to get O-U-T, *out* of this building.

The school splits up to go on three different field trips, all on the same day. This year, the first and second graders were going to the Aquarium, and the fifth and sixth graders were going to the Museum of Science.

The third and fourth graders were going to Plimoth Plantation. We had been preparing for it all year. In the fall, we raised money by having a talent show and a bike rally. This winter we read so many books and watched so many videos that we became experts about the Pilgrims and the Wampanoag Native People. I still had some questions, though.

"So is this a looking place, or a doing place?" I asked as our teacher handed out the field trip permission slips.

"Looking or doing?" he repeated. "What does that mean?"

"Are we going to be *looking* at Ye Olden Times stuff, or *doing* Ye Olden Times stuff?"

My second grade teacher had been nuts about Ye Olden Days *looking* stuff. Let me tell you, I do not ever want to see another calico bonnet in my life. Only one thing last year was a *doing* thing, but even that was a disappointment. Here is the big johnnycake lesson: *Make pancakes. Eat them without syrup.* That is all, and I am not even kidding.

"Some of both," Mr. D'Matz answered.

"Okay, I pick the doing things," I decided right away.

"Me, too!" said Waylon. "I'm on the doing things side."

"Me, too!" said Willy and Lilly and Rasheed and Maria and Joe and Charlie and everybody else in the class.

Mr. D'Matz laughed. "Well, that's good information, I guess. Lots of hands-on activities for my class. I'll see that our guide gets the message. Now, I need these permission slips back by Wednesday. Plimoth Plantation is an hour away. We'll be leaving right at eight o'clock, so if you walk or get driven to school, make sure you are not late on Thursday."

Maria raised her hand to ask how we were going to get there.

"Buses," our teacher said. "You'll sit with your partner, on the same bus, both ways."

And then I thought of something important. "Which buses?" I asked. "Not Bus Seven, right?"

All at once, kids began to pretend-gag. "The Cloud! Gaaaccckkk! Not The Cloud . . ." kids moaned.

"The Cloud?" Mr. D'Matz asked.

Kids were falling out of their seats now, pretending they were dying from just thinking about how smelly Bus Seven was. Well, all the kids except for Kyla and Charlie. They both put their heads down on their desks. They had to take Bus Seven every day.

I have only taken Bus Seven one time, but one time was enough, let me tell you. If you took all the terrible-smelling things you could think of and mixed them together and let them rot for a good long time, it would smell like roses compared to The Cloud. The smell gets worse with every step you take toward the back of the bus, except that it gets a little better at the very last row, but that might be just because at the very last row you can smell the exhaust. Bus exhaust smells like roses too, compared to The Cloud.

Our teacher raised his hand over his head, and

everyone finally quieted down. "We need to get a lot of work done this week if we're going to go on a field trip Thursday," he said. "Please take out your Fraction Blaster packets, and let's forget about Bus Seven."

We took out our Fraction Blaster packets, but nobody forgot about Bus Seven.

"I had turtles once," Joe said as soon as we were out at recess. "When I forgot to clean their tank for a really long time, it smelled like The Cloud. My mother made me give them away because of that smell. The only people we could find to take them lived in Connecticut,

27

but my mother said, 'No problem! We'll deliver!' I bet there are turtles on that bus."

Charlie shook his head. "No. What it smells like is that cheese that smells like feet."

"No," said Waylon. "What it smells like is feet that smell like that cheese that smells like feet."

I left my classmates arguing and went over to the pine tree in the corner of the playground. All that Bus Seven talk had made my nose want to smell something good. I sat on the pine needles under the tree, taking nice deep sniffs and thinking about my apple tree. Someday it would be as big as this pine tree. Someday people would sit under it and enjoy how nice it smelled, especially in the spring when it would be covered with blossoms.

Before I went back to the group, I gathered a few pine needles to keep in my pocket in case the kids weren't finished talking about The Cloud.

They weren't.

"No," Morris-Boris was saying. "What it smells like is this: If you find cat throw-up lying on the sidewalk on a hot day and you wrap it in one of your socks after you've been out playing soccer, and then you accidentally stuff the cat throw-up sock into the chimney of your sister's dollhouse, and then hide the dollhouse in the back of your closet for six months and then accidentally put it back in your sister's room . . . that's what it smells like."

We all stared at Morris-Boris. I knew everyone was thinking the same thing: Morris-Boris was the nicest person in our whole class, maybe even the whole school.

"You did that? You?" I asked. "You really did that to your sister?"

Now Morris-Boris looked shocked. "Of *course* not!" he said. "I don't even *have* a sister. I was just saying The Cloud smells like *if* you did all that."

Just then the recess-is-over bell rang. The kids kept on arguing about the smell as we filed inside.

"No," Adrian said as he hung up his jacket. "It smells like once, after my dog ate an entire—"

Our teacher held up both his *Stop!* hands. "Okay, okay, that's enough. I get the picture," he said. "I'll send a note along to the bus company, have them look into the problem."

3

From the back, my mom still looks like my mom. But from the front, these days, she looks like a pear, which is lucky for her because I am even better at drawing fruit than people. When I got home from school Monday afternoon, she looked so round I grabbed my sketchbook to make a picture. I drew a floating pear, and then drew overalls on it. Then I put my mom's head on the stem, added arms and legs, and erased the leaf coming off her shoulder. Here is a picture of that:

When I showed the drawing to my mother, she
went into her bedroom to look at herself in the
mirror. I heard her sigh a couple of times. "You're
right," she said when she came back. "I look like
a pear."

That is how good of an artist I am: in my drawings, people even know what fruit they are.

My mom lowered herself onto the couch. She patted her belly, which looked like it had a watermelon strapped to it, and sighed again. "I miss my waist."

I looked at my drawing, and then at my mom's belly, trying to figure something out. "Mom, where do all your guts go? Like your stomach. Or your lungs."

My mom laughed. "Oh, everything's still in here. The baby does make things a little crowded, though. A little squashed. And it's a good thing skin is so stretchy, because this little guy or girl is still growing."

I erased the clogs from my mom's feet and drew on her favorite shoes—green sparkly dragonfly high heels—which she can't wear anymore because of having pregnant feet. Then I put down my pencil. "I still can't decide what I want it to be," I said. "If it's a boy, then there will be three people on the boy team. If it's a girl, we'll have another one on the girl team, but it won't be just you and me anymore. I don't know which is better."

"What do you mean? You think there are teams in this family?"

"Of course. You and me, and Dad and Watercress."

"First of all, your brother's name is not Watercress. And second of all, is that really how it feels to you? As if we're on different teams?"

"Well . . ." I said slowly, since suddenly I didn't know if it did or it didn't.

My mom rolled over on the couch to face me. "Maybe you could think of our family as one team, together," she said. "But we're not the kind of team that's against anybody." She raised herself up. "And it's the same for all people!" she said, her voice getting higher. "There's no 'us against them.' We're ALL us! And we're ALL them!"

I scrambled to my feet. When my mom gets like this, my dad calls it "going crunchy." He says it's something he really likes about her—that she cares so much about things being fair and right. But I have noticed that he does exactly the same thing

I do when she starts going crunchy, which is: get out of the room. But before I could escape all the way, she asked me a good question.

"Clementine, can you think of a single reason girls and boys would be on different teams?"

I turned at the doorway.

"Don't you think all people want the same things?" she went on. "Boys *and* girls? I'm talking about the big things, the basics. Like . . . freedom, and the right to a good place to live."

"You mean like a nice home?"

"I meant a nice planet, but sure, like a nice home. Clean and safe and comfortable. Do you think boys and girls are on different teams about wanting that? Or how about the chance to grow up to be whatever you want? Like the chance to be a musician. Or a carpenter. Or a nurse. It shouldn't matter if you're a girl or a boy for any of that, should it?"

I sighed and sat down on the arm of the couch. This was going to take a while.

"And since everyone wants to eat food, don't you think both girls and boys should help prepare it? We're not on different teams about that, right?"

Thinking about food made me remember about Thursday, about how bad it was going to be to have to eat with the fourth graders. My mom was wrong that people weren't on different teams against each other. The fourth graders and the third graders sure were.

"So you see?" my mom was saying. "Human beings aren't on different teams, are they?"

I figured my mom had it bad enough with her lungs being squashed without having her heart crushed too. So I just said, "Sure, I guess. Thanks for explaining that." Then I picked up my drawing and erased the pencil lines down my mom's sides.

I redrew them so they went in instead of out at the middle, even though usually I like to draw things the true way they are. Then I signed my drawing and gave it to her.

"Anyway," I said, "I still don't know which I want the baby to be."

"Just as well," my mother said. "We don't get to decide anyway." She looked at my drawing and smiled. "I appreciate the waist," she said. "If we *were* on teams, Clementine, I'd make you the captain of mine."

Just then Snap Pea woke up from his nap, and my mother went in to get him. "I'm going to check on my apple tree," I called out. I filled the watering can and left.

In the lobby, I found my father, cleaning out the display case.

I put the watering can down. "What are we decorating for this month?"

"Oh, April is jam-packed," my dad said. "It's National Poetry Month, National Welding Month, National Humor Month, and a whole bunch more. It was a tough choice."

"So what did you decide?"

My dad pointed to a cardboard box on the floor next to a pile of plastic branches. It was full of brown plastic nuts.

"National Pecan Month," my dad said. "I'm going to stick them onto these branches."

"Really?" I asked. "Pecans get their own month?"

"The pecan is the only nut tree native to North America," said my dad. "Of course it gets its own month. Its own day, too—the fourteenth is National Pecan Day."

My dad handed me his list of holidays. Besides the monthly ones, he decorates for some of the daily ones, too. He lets me choose one each month.

"April *is* packed," I said. "And confusing. The fourth is Tell-A-Lie-Day, but the thirtieth is National Honesty Day." I read down the list. As usual, the not-choosing part was the worst. Blame-Someone-Else Day, Jugglers' Day, and Cheeseball Day were all hard to pass up. But then I found the perfect one. "April eighth is National Draw-A-Bird Day. I'll do that one."

We got to work sticking the nuts onto the branches. Just as I hung up a PECANS ARE POPPING! sign, the elevator gears whirred behind us.

I dropped the tape and spun around, because elevator doors are like game-show prize doors: until they open, you never know what valuable stuff is hiding behind them. Okay, fine—in our building, it's usually just the same old people, riding up and down from their condos. But once I thought I recognized a man from the Post Office's Most Wanted poster, and once I definitely saw a woman carrying a mannequin's leg in a grocery bag, so you never know.

Also, I watch the elevator doors because sometimes it is Mitchell who gets out. Which does N-O-T, *not* mean he is my boyfriend.

And this time it was Mitchell! He was smiling

even harder than usual when he got out of the elevator. Then I saw who was with him.

"Hey, what are you doing here?" I asked.

"Stuff," Mitchell said.

"I was asking Waylon," I said. "Waylon, what are you doing here?"

"Stuff," Waylon said, glancing up at Mitchell and covering a giggle.

A couple of months ago, when Waylon was over to work on our science project, I introduced him to Mitchell. Since then they have been getting together all the time. They act like they have this big secret project going, but I know that all it is, is baseball. Waylon is teaching Mitchell the scienciness of it, and Mitchell is teaching him how to actually play.

Waylon and Mitchell high-fived their mitts.

"We're not on teams, you know," I said.

"Yeah, we are," Mitchell said. "Team Vector!"

He and Waylon bumped mitts again, and then they left.

"You're not on a team together against me," I said. To myself.

The elevator doors opened again. This time it was my mother and Swiss Chard. Mom charged over to take a closer look at our decorations. She grabbed hold of her hair and shook her head with it, as if she was so upset her neck wouldn't even do that job for her. "What on earth . . . ? Never seen anything . . . Lobby full of plastic . . ." she sputtered.

"I know," my dad said. "It's so beautiful I'm practically speechless too. National Pecan Month might be my finest creation."

"Where did you even *get* plastic pecans?" my mom asked. She shuddered and backed away from the display case, because she feels about plastic the way Margaret feels about germs.

My dad beamed. "It wasn't easy, let me tell you. I've been searching for years. First, I tried—"

My mom put up both hands. "Never mind. I can't bear to hear it. But please—how about a bowl of actual pecans if it's Pecan Month? How about putting out a bowl of real, crack-them-and-eat-them, actual nuts? Isn't that a better way to

celebrate? I could go
to the store right now
and get some. . . ."

"Good idea," Dad said to my mom. He put a
hand on my shoulder and picked up my brother.
"I've got these two nuts. You go get us some
actual pecans."

"Are you going to start decorating the lobby
with real things now?" I asked when my mom was
gone. "What about the fire codes?"

He smiled down at me. "Probably not. But your
mom was about to go crunchy on us. It's a beautiful day out, and I thought she would enjoy a walk.

Besides, a bowl of nuts is a nice idea. People will eat them."

"Dad, why do you call it 'going crunchy' when Mom gets like that?"

My dad sat down on the lobby bench with Coleslaw on his lap and patted the space beside him. "Did I ever tell you the story of how I first fell in love with your mother?"

I sat down because my dad has about a hundred stories that end with "I fell in love with your mother that day," and they're all good.

"Well," he said, "we were talking to some friends outside the library. Her hair was flying around and her arms were waving in the air—she was so worked up she was practically levitating. She looked so pretty I could barely pay attention to what she was saying—I just knew it was something about the big problem of food not being crunchy enough. I didn't really see how the world

48

would be a better place with crunchier food, but I fell in love with your mother that day."

"But, Dad," I reminded him, "what about the time she made you empty the vacuum cleaner bag because she thought you'd sucked up an ant? I thought you fell in love with her then. And what about when she spit the cherry pits?"

"Well, sure," my dad said. "I fell in love with that woman *lots* of times!"

At school Tuesday morning, after the "Yet?" and "Not yet" stuff, I had a big surprise. A girl with short black hair and a purple backpack was standing on the other side of Mr. D'Matz's desk.

When we were all in our seats, our teacher said, "Class, please say hello to our new student, Olive. I know I can count on you to make her feel welcome."

Mr. D'Matz made us introduce ourselves, and then he led Olive to the empty desk in the back of the room. When he told her she could put her stuff inside, we all gasped: nobody had used that desk since Baxter left in September.

Even though he had only been with us for a few days, I really missed Baxter, and not just because he'd let you look at his webbed toes as long as you wanted for only a quarter. He pried the legs off his chair, loosened the screws on the coat hooks so our jackets fell down all morning, and filled the classroom soap dispenser with creamed corn from lunch. And that was just the first day of school.

Because I have extra-great hearing, I overheard what our teacher said to Principal Rice out in the hall when he handed Baxter over to her that afternoon: "He certainly is a resourceful young man."

Okay, fine—I had to go up and sharpen my pencil with my ear stretched out to the cracked-open door to overhear that.

"'Resourceful' is an understatement," I overheard Mrs. Rice say when she returned him half an hour later.

"Clementine, what are you doing?" my teacher asked when he came back into the classroom with Baxter.

I held up my pencil, which was by now sharpened on both ends. "And excuse me, I please need to use the dictionary, thank you." I thumbed through it until I found "resourceful." It means "able to use any ways and means available to achieve goals."

And our teacher and Mrs. Rice were right: Baxter sure was resourceful.

As we were waiting for the buses after school, Baxter told us that in the half hour he had been gone, he had managed to steal the minute hand from Mrs. Rice's principal clock, and reverse the hot and cold faucets in the grown-ups-only bathroom. So he had achieved some goals, all right.

The question I had was about his "ways and means available."

"Wow, so you bring tools to school?" I asked him.

Baxter smirked. "Tools are for amateurs." He slid a plastic bag from his backpack and held it out. Inside were a Popsicle stick, a paper clip, a pack of gum, a couple of thumbtacks, and a bunch of rubber bands. "I'm a professional. I can take apart anything with just what I've got in this bag."

Some of the kids didn't believe him. "You couldn't have done all that with Mrs. Rice right there. I think you're lying," Charlie had said on the bus to school the next day. In return, Baxter had stolen Charlie's sandwich out of his lunchbox and replaced it with a rubber frog. This made Charlie really mad when he found out about it at lunch. "It was Egguna!" he wailed. "I invented it! Egg salad and tuna fish! He's a liar *and* a thief!"

Nobody else was mad at Baxter, and we didn't care if he was lying or not. We just liked having him around. But then, three days later, he was gone.

"Baxter moved to Kansas," I'd told Margaret on the bus that afternoon.

"Ha," she snorted. "That's a good one. He probably got arrested. A *prison* is probably where he moved to."

When I told my classmates what Margaret had said, they all agreed with me that this was good news: Baxter would have no problem busting out of any prison in the world. He'd be back soon with some pretty good stories, we figured. All year long we'd been keeping an eye on his empty desk.

But now this new Olive-girl was sitting there.

At recess, everybody crowded around to find out if she was as interesting as Baxter.

"Can you use your thumbnail as a screwdriver?" asked Willy.

"Can you pop a lock with a paper clip?" asked Charlie.

Olive shook her head no to both of those.

"Have you ever been in prison?" I asked.

"No," Olive said. "Never."

She was looking kind of embarrassed by now, so I gave her a cheer-up smile.

"Me neither," I admitted. "And I can't do *any* of the great stuff Baxter could."

Hearing that we had this in common seemed to perk Olive up.

"And hey, Clementine," she said, "we both have food names too!"

I stopped to think about this. All my life I have wished I didn't have a food name. I call my brother different vegetable names to make it fair. But it's still not. "Nobody else got a food name," I tell my parents, over and over. "I'm the only one." And I was—except for Mrs. Rice, who didn't count because it was her last name. But now, finally, here was another kid with a first name that was a food!

And suddenly, I wasn't so sure I wanted to share. I turned back to Olive.

"Do you ever wish you had a regular name?" I asked.

Olive looked surprised. "Of course not. Olive is a great name. Plus, it's also a language."

All nineteen heads, including mine, snapped to attention at that.

"Olive-language," Olive said. "I invented it. You put 'olive' into every syllable you say." She pointed to her shoes and said, "Sholivoos." She pointed to Willy's cap and said, "Colivap." Then she pointed to my jacket and said, "Jolivackolivet."

All the kids acted as if this was the most amazing miracle anyone could do in the whole world. They began naming the things around us in her language: "Trolivee!" "Swoliving solivet!" "Dolivodge bolivall!"

"My name is great too," I interrupted.

Nobody even looked back at me.

"Clementine is a language too, you know."

A couple of kids glanced at me.

I decided to say "A *secret* language!" in my new language, but I had to stop to invent one first. What I invented is this: put the word "clementine" into every syllable you say. I practiced Clementine-language in my head, and let me tell you, it was not easy. By the time I was ready to say the first word—"Se-clementine-cre-clementine-et"—all the kids had gathered around Olive again.

"Wow," Lilly sighed. "Talking Olive makes you sound like you come from another country!"

"Well, so what," I said. "My language makes you sound like you come from another *planet*."

Olive spun around. "What planet?"

"Zephon," I made up right away. This is a lucky thing about me: stuff comes out of my mouth without me even having to think about it! "Planet Zephon. You wouldn't like it there, Olive. It's a place where they don't have olives."

When I got home from school, I went right into the kitchen for a snack. Margaret had spent the whole bus ride home re-reminding me about the eating-sounds rule, and it had made me hungry for really loud food. I grabbed a granola bar from the cupboard and took a big, crunching bite.

Immediately my cat, Moisturizer, came skittering into the kitchen to see if what I was eating was Kat Krunchies. When he saw it was just human

food, he turned his nose up and began playing the new game he invented: I Am NOT Interested in You!

I walked over to the window above the sink and

pretended to be fascinated by the feet walking by on the sidewalk. In a second, I heard his soft paws coming over to stop beside me. But when I looked down, he yawned to show me how not-interested in me he was. I sat down at the table, and then he sauntered over to the table too, as if it was just a big coincidence that we both needed to be there. When I looked over to say hi to him, he flopped down and stared at his tail, as if he had no idea how this miraculous toy had become attached to his back.

Just then, my mother came into the kitchen. She didn't say "Hi, honey, how was your day?" the way she usually does. Instead, she yanked open the refrigerator and stared into it exactly the way a starving wolf stares into an empty rabbit hole, which I saw on the Nature Channel once, except Mom was not actually drooling. I knew what this meant: my mother was having a craving.

When you are pregnant you get to eat whatever you want, together with whatever else you want, whenever you want it, just by saying the magic words "I'm having a craving." What you always hear about is pickles and ice cream, but my mother has not craved either of those things, not even separately. My father buys them every week just in case, though. At the end of the week, he sits down with a gigantic bowl of ice cream and a side dish of pickles, so he can use them up. "The things I do for your mother," he says. Then he goes to get a fresh supply of pickles and ice cream, and also raw clams, which is what my mother is actually craving.

"There are no clams in here," my mother wailed now, so loudly that Mrs. Jacoby on the top floor probably heard her. "I will go out of my mind if I can't have some clams *right now!*"

My dad came skidding into the kitchen and patted my mom's shoulder. "You ate a whole platter of them yesterday," he reminded her gently. "Dear."

My mom spun around to give him a look that said she was N-O-T, *not* kidding about needing raw clams right now. My dad threw his palms up and backed away. Then he gestured for me to meet him at the front door. We put on our Red Sox caps, which Mitchell insists we wear once baseball season opens, and headed out to the fish market.

"Now . . . clams," he said, when we were outside. "This is a really good sign, let me tell you. This means your little brother or sister is going to have a rock-hard head, like a clamshell. Our little guy's going to be able to split firewood with a head like that. He or she will be able to butt right through a cement wall. A torpedo-head like that's going to come in awfully handy for our family."

"What did Mom crave when she was pregnant with me?" I asked, even though I already knew the answer.

"Pineapple," my dad said. "She'd eat it with anything. Pineapple with peanut butter, pineapple with mustard, pineapple with chili. She couldn't get enough of it."

"And that's how you knew I'd be sweet," I said, the way I always do.

"Don't be ridiculous, Clementine!" my father said, the way he always does. He rapped the top of my head with his knuckles. "That's how we knew you'd have spiky green skin!"

CHAPTER
5

Wednesday morning, we had oatmeal for break-fast. "Tell me if you can hear me eating this," I said to my brother. I took a tiny mouse-nibble, sealed my lips tight around it, and swallowed as quietly as I could.

My brother bugged his eyes and clapped his hands over his ears as though the jackhammers from Boston Common had started up again, extra volume. I glared at him, which made him laugh so hard he tipped out of his chair.

One way my brother is like my father is that he

thinks he is a comedian. One way he is N-O-T, *not* like my father is that he is never funny.

"Never mind," I told him. "You'll have to eat with the fourth graders one day, and you won't be laughing then."

The whole bus ride to school, Margaret re-warned me about the rule. Just hearing about all the food sounds that could get me in trouble practically gave me a nervous breakdown. Things got worse when I went into my classroom.

After my teacher and I said "Yet?" and "Not yet," he called me up to his desk. "Clementine, I've arranged for you to partner with Olive for the field trip tomorrow," he said.

"I can't. I'm already being partners with Margaret. I promised her," I said. "So . . . sorry."

"Margaret's teacher will see to getting her another partner," Mr. D'Matz said. "I need someone reliable to partner with our new student."

"Why me?" I asked. "Why not Willy, or Lilly? Why not Willy and Lilly together?" Although actually, I knew why not Willy and Lilly together —Lilly is too busy bossing Willy to boss a new person.

"It's a compliment, Clementine," my teacher said. "I know you'll do a good job of making Olive feel comfortable on the field trip."

I wanted to ask, *What about Margaret? What about me? Now who's going to make us feel comfortable on the field trip?* But Mr. D'Matz was already standing up and collecting permission slips. Instead, when he asked for someone to deliver them to the office, I launched my hand like a rocket.

After I dropped the permission slips off, I knocked on the principal's door. Mrs. Rice stuck out her hand for the note from my teacher I usually have when I visit her, but I shook my head. "I'm here to volunteer to stay at school tomorrow and spy on the party for you."

"The party?" Mrs. Rice asked. "What party is that?"

"The one the lunchroom ladies and the custodians are going to have. You know. With all the great food the lunchroom ladies hide from us."

"No, I don't know about any party tomorrow," Principal Rice said. "But what I *do* know about tomorrow is that it's your field trip."

I heaved a tragedy sigh. "It's too bad I'll miss it. But the lunchroom ladies and the custodians are

70

probably going to play poker and dance around," I said, making my voice extra tragic. "Maybe the librarian, too. And the nurse. Maybe there will even be kissing at the party. You know what spring does to people. I'd better stay and watch for you. My friend Margaret can stay too."

"Clementine, the cafeteria is closed tomorrow, and all the staff have the day off. Now, I understand you're going to buddy-up with our newest student on the field trip. Your teacher is counting on you. I think he's made a wise choice."

Suddenly my head was too tired to pretend anymore. It dropped down to Mrs. Rice's desk, which I think should have a pillow on it, because talking to her makes my head tired a lot.

"Is something wrong, Clementine?" Mrs. Rice asked.

I rolled my head over so my mouth could move. "Margaret can't touch anything that might make her dirty," I said. "She needs me to be with her so I can do all the doing things for her. Also, I need Margaret with me because I can't do silent eating. I've been practicing at home, and I just can't do it." I lifted my still-tired head to look at her. "And anyway, I don't even *want* to do silent eating. Why do I have to care about something stupid

like that? I want to stay in third grade forever."

Principal Rice rested her cheek on her hand. "You're not excited to be a fourth grader next fall?" she asked. "What's going on?"

I explained everything that Margaret had explained to me about the fourth grade rule. I even added the horror-faces Margaret had made that

had scared me so much, so she would understand.

But when I was finished, Mrs. Rice only shrugged. "I agree with you about that rule. What do you think you should do?"

Which meant that even though she was the boss of everybody in the school, she didn't have any good ideas about not getting bossed by other people. So I pushed in the chair and told her I was all done being there.

"See you tomorrow," Principal Rice said.

"Okay, fine," I said. But it wasn't.

When I got home from school, I plunked myself next to the window to look for birds to draw for National Draw-A-Bird Day. No matter what's wrong, making art always makes me feel better. Right away I saw something that would make a great picture: a pigeon struggling to peck apart a bagel out on the sidewalk. Mrs. Jacoby on the seventh floor dumped Cheerios out for the pigeons every day, and this pigeon looked like he was thinking, *Wow, this one is gigantic!*

I borrowed a big piece of paper from my mom,

who was working on her own drawing, and lay down on the floor to work. Let me tell you, it is not easy drawing the "I must be dreaming!" face on a pigeon, even for someone like me, who is practically a famous artist. The beak kept looking all cribbled up. As I was erasing it for the third time, my father stuck his head into the living room.

"Clementine," he said, "we've had a call from the Pentagon."

I jumped up and saluted. "We'd better go," I answered.

My mother threw her hands up in the air. "What is it with you two and this Pentagon joke, lately?" she cried. "I don't get it."

"Sorry, top secret mission," I told her. "National security."

My mom shook her head, and I followed my dad out to the basement. We went into the workshop, and I closed the door behind us. "You can't be too careful when you're working on the Pentagon," I reminded him.

My mom thinks we are kidding when we talk about the Pentagon, but the real joke is that we're not. The Pentagon is an actual thing—just not the one near Washington that's filled with army people. Our Pentagon is a secret present my dad and I are building to celebrate the new baby coming. Our Pentagon is a table, one that will be just right for our new family because it has five sides, one for everybody.

It is not that easy building a five-sided table, let me tell you. The big problem is the corner angles—they aren't square, the way they are on regular tables. I was the one who finally figured it out. "Look, Dad," I said after we'd stared at the picture in my math book for a while. "A pentagon is really just three triangles, put together."

My dad turned the book around and around, but

he still didn't see it. So I drew it out on a piece of paper.

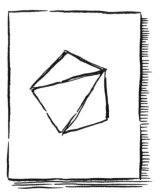

My dad ruffled up my hair and grinned when he understood. "Genius kid," he laughed. "So a triangle has a hundred and eighty degrees, and there are three, which means . . ."

"Five hundred and forty," I prompted. "A pentagon's corners add up to five hundred and forty degrees."

"I think you're right! And five hundred and forty degrees, divided by five is . . ."

"A hundred and eight degrees," I figured out.

"Genius kid," he said again, nodding. "I got me a genius kid."

My dad pulled the blanket off the Pentagon. It wasn't a table yet, but you could tell that's what it was going to be soon. The five legs were ready,

cut the same length, and sanded until they were smooth. The top was a beautiful piece of wood we had rubbed with oil.

"What are we doing today?" I asked.

"Assembling the skirt," my dad said. "The table skirt is made of the boards that run perpendicular to the tabletop, parallel to the perimeter, just beneath it . . ."

He kept going with his la-de-blah-blah carpentry words, but I studied the plans instead.

"I get it," I interrupted him. "The skirt is the part that hangs down under the top *like a skirt*. That the legs stick out from, *like a skirt*."

"Well," my dad said—"well, yes! That's a better way to say it, I guess. Now, what we're going to need are a saw and a drill and a pencil and some clamps."

We buckled on our tool belts and got to work.

Let me tell you, it is very hard to hold boards together to clamp them and then mark them and drill the holes. Finally I dropped the drill. "I can't do it!" I cried. "My hands are too confused!"

"One at a time," my dad said. "One tool. One hand. One piece of wood. One step. One at a time."

I held the board with one hand. My dad placed the ruler over it. With my other hand I marked the spot to drill. And my dad was right. One tool, one piece of wood, one step at a time, we built the Pentagon's skirt.

Just as I was hanging up my tool belt beside my dad's, I heard the elevator clunk to a stop. My dad and I threw the cover over the Pentagon and closed the workshop door behind us.

It was Margaret. She had a pinched-down, don't-cry mouth, and she nodded at my apartment door without saying anything. I let her in, and then followed her to my bedroom.

"What's wrong?" I asked.

Margaret sank down onto my bed without even placing a germ-protective towel on the bedspread, something I had never seen before. "My mother and Alan aren't just twitterpated," she said. "They're getting married! And Alan's moving in! Mitchell only said, 'Oh, cool,' and then went off to baseball practice, as if it was no big deal. But it *is* a big deal. It's terrible!"

"But I thought you didn't mind Alan anymore," I said.

"I'm used to him now," Margaret said. "It's not *him* I mind moving in with us. It's his pipe. Alan's pipe will be living at my house, Clementine! Every time I touch something, I'm going to have to worry about pipe germs crawling around on me. Things were fine the way they were. Why does my mother have to go and change everything?"

This winter, when I'd found out about our new baby coming, I'd felt the same way: NO THANKS TO CHANGE!

"Yep, change is part bad," my dad had admitted. "But it's part good, too," he'd said. "It's up to us to figure out which part to concentrate on."

"Well," I said now to Margaret, "are there any good parts to Alan's moving in?"

Margaret scrunched her eyes closed and thought hard. "Alan hates baseball," she said finally. "My mother and Mitchell are obsessed with it. Now at least we'll be on even teams for television watching. Hey! Maybe we'll get to watch *The Neat Squad* some nights instead of the Red Sox."

Margaret's favorite television show is about a team of professional organizers who go into people's messy houses and straighten them up while they are away, as if that would be a wonderful surprise to anybody. Once, my father had joked that he was going to call up that show and tell them about my bedroom, and I stopped speaking to him for a day and a half.

Anyway, I didn't think someone who left his pipe around everywhere was going to vote to watch a show called *The Neat Squad*.

"Can you think of any other good things about them getting married?" I asked.

Margaret said, "Hmm, hmmmm," so long that I started to give up hope. But then she came up with something. "When my parents were married, they never kissed. Maybe my mother and Alan will stop kissing once they get married." Margaret looked like she was trying hard to cheer herself up with this idea, so I didn't tell her the bad news: my parents were married, and they kissed all the time.

Margaret got up and walked over to my bureau. She stood there looking over my stuff, her hands twitching.

I have a lot of different sections, like the fruit that's my name. Watching Margaret at my bureau, half of my Clementine sections wanted to say, *Don't touch anything!* But the other half of them were thinking, *Oh, let her play* Neat Squad *on your bureau if it will make her happy.* Luckily, there was a knock at my door before I had to decide which half should win.

It was my dad. He handed Margaret the photo he'd taken of her in the Common on Sunday. "Thought you might like a copy of this," he said.

Margaret's whole body seemed to smile, looking at that picture. Which gave me a great idea.

After she left, I got out my drawing of the pigeon with the bagel. I flipped it over and started

on a new drawing. It took a long time, because I
gave each of the brass ducklings their own sparkle
rays, and then put a bunch on Margaret, too, so she
looked like the sun. But when it was finished, it was
beautiful. And although it was still a few days until
National Draw-A-Bird Day, my dad and I went up
to the lobby and taped it next to the display case.

CHAPTER
6

Thursday morning, my eyelids snapped open like cartoon window shades. If I could stay safe from the fourth graders, this was going to be a great day! I jumped out of bed and raced into the kitchen to pack my lunch. But my mother was already up, and she was doing it. "Mom, no!" I cried. "No crackers! No carrots! And no apple!"

"Why not?" she asked, zipping the carrots into a bag. "You like them."

"I like them, but I can't *eat* them! Those things make eating sounds you could hear on Mars."

"Clementine, what are you talking about?"
She took out some almond butter.

"And no almond butter! Almond butter makes snicking! This trip is with the fourth graders, Mom. They have a rule about eating sounds. No crunching, no chewing, no slurping, no glugging, and definitely no snicking."

My dad came in then, with my brother in his arms. "There is a rule about eating sounds?" he asked.

"Of course," I said. And then I explained to my parents everything Margaret had warned me about.

When I was finished, my dad looked up from stirring yogurt into my brother's cereal. "Who made this rule?" he asked.

"Dad. I already said. The fourth graders. First the mean ones, and now all of them."

"Yes, but who are these people? The sound police?"

"Dad, they're the fourth graders! They're the

bosses of the whole school, because they're the oldest. Except for the fifth and sixth graders, but they don't count because they're locked up on the second floor."

"But who *are* they, Clementine?" my dad asked again. My brother stared at him as if even he knew that was a dumb question.

My father has trouble paying attention. I used to have trouble paying attention too. Okay, fine—I still have trouble paying attention.

I went over to my dad, looked right into his eyes, and smiled. "Dad," I said in a really kind

voice—the voice I wish people would use on me when I'm having trouble paying attention—"the fourth graders are Margaret and the other *fourth graders.*"

"But aren't they just kids? Kids who used to be third graders like you? I think that's what your father's asking," my mother said. "And who will be the fourth graders next year?"

"The third graders will be! We will! Me!" And then I stopped. "Oh," I said.

"Exactly," my mom said. "And would you make a rule like that?"

"Of course not!" I said. "We'll probably make a new rule. One that says you have to be as loud as you can when you're eating."

My dad put my brother's cereal down in front of him. "Food is a big deal, Clementine," he said. "Most people would be happy just to have enough of it. So maybe you won't make any rules about eating. In fact, maybe you won't make any rules at all."

Sometimes he has trouble staying serious.

"Dad," I reminded him, "making rules is the whole point of being a fourth grader."

My dad went off to work, my mom left to get Kohlrabi dressed, and I repacked my lunch.

I saw my dad again in the lobby as I was leaving. "Got your homework, Sport?" he asked.

"No homework," I said. "Field trip."

"Oh, right." He patted my backpack. "Well, then, you've got plenty of room in here." He unzipped it and tossed in a package of pecans. "Courtesy of the Condo Association. Your mom went a little overboard, a little extra-crunchy. Share them, and have fun today."

I didn't point out to him how dangerously loud nuts were, because just then, the elevator doors opened. Margaret stepped out. She pointed at me.

"You'll make him an ashtray," she said. "I'll give it to him and say, 'Alan, your pipe lives *here.*'"

"That's a really good solution, Margaret!" I said. And it was, because we'd all get to do what we loved most: I'd get to do an art project, Margaret would get to make a rule, and Alan would get to smoke his pipe.

Then I pointed at the drawing I'd done of her with the shiny duck statues.

Margaret looked. "Oh!" she said. "Oh, oh, oh!" With each "Oh!" she seemed to sprout her own sparkle rays. She stood there "Oh!"-ing and sprouting sparkle rays so long I worried we were going to miss the bus.

"Remember, you said I could clean the lobby this weekend," she called out to my dad as I pulled her past him. "The steps, too, okay?"

My dad said okay, and then I dragged Margaret out the door. On the bus I showed her my lunch.

"There's no mayonnaise on this chicken sandwich, is there?" she asked me.

"Of course not," I said. "Snicking."

She nodded at the string cheese and the raisins, threw in a bunch of her hand wipes, then finally she said, "Okay. But remember: keep your mouth closed."

I shut my lunch box. "Margaret, what are you going to do next year, when you're in fifth grade?"

Margaret slumped over, as though her head was suddenly too heavy for her neck. "I wish I could stay in fourth grade forever," she admitted. "You wouldn't believe the stories Mitchell tells me about that second floor. He says it's a miracle any of the fifth graders survive."

"Well, what I meant was, what are you going to do about not making the rules anymore?"

Margaret's head fell down even farther. "I don't know," she mumbled into her lap. "My life will be over."

When we got to school, we went inside to our classrooms as usual. But all we did was take attendance and listen for the three hundredth time about how to behave on a field trip so we wouldn't make our school embarrassed. I asked my teacher "Yet?" and he answered "Not yet," and then we lined up to go right back outside.

Pretty soon the whole school was there. Our teachers read off partners and assigned us to groups for the buses.

Kyla elbowed me. She pointed to one of the buses waiting in the line.

"What?" I asked. "Those are the buses. What?" And then I understood. "Oh, no. Oh, no," I said. "Kyla, is it . . . ?"

Kyla nodded. The word passed around until everyone was staring at Bus Seven. You could practically see the smell-rays pulsing out of it.

"Cheer up," I told our group. "Maybe it's here for the big kids."

The fifth and sixth graders climbed onto Bus Five and Bus One and took off for the Museum of Science.

Bus Seven sat lurking at the back of the parking

lot like a stink bomb waiting to explode.

"Cheer up," I said. "Maybe it's here for the little kids."

A few minutes later the first and second graders got shoveled onto Bus Eleven and Bus Four and left for the Aquarium.

"Cheer up," I said to my group. "It's probably here for our other group."

Except by now even I knew what was going to happen. And sure enough, the other group of third and fourth graders practically danced onto Bus Three, they were so happy to be avoiding The Cloud.

And Bus Seven pulled up in front of us. If you have ever watched prisoners walking the plank on a pirate show, you will know how we climbed onto that bus.

The strongest kids wrestled their way into the front seats, farthest away from The Cloud. Olive and I got stuck with the second-to-last row, where The Cloud was really bad. Willy and Lilly were in front of us, Maria and Rasheed were across the aisle, and Margaret and Amanda Lee took the back row.

Right away, everyone started gagging and groaning. I didn't know which was worse—the smell, or the noise of the kids complaining about the smell. I pressed my nose against the glass and clapped my hands over my ears.

The door cranked open, and Mrs. Rice climbed onto the bus. She began making her way down the aisle, staring each kid in the eyes until he or she went silent. Even though I am not going to be a principal when I grow up, I'm going to go to principal school so I can learn some of the great tricks they teach there.

When Principal Rice came to our row, I zipped my lips and plugged my fingers into my ears to show her we were on the same team about the noise. Then I pinched my nose and pretended to faint, to let her know it still smelled gross, though. Mrs. Rice nodded at Olive and me for being quiet, and then turned her stare onto Maria and Rasheed.

And that is when I saw something I had never seen in my entire life: Mrs. Rice was not wearing her principal shoes! Instead, her feet were strapped into some navy blue puffy things. I climbed over the back of Olive's seat and hung down to get a better look. I think the things on her feet were supposed to be sandals, but what they looked like was . . . car seats!

I wanted to ask her if they made her feet feel like

they wanted to go for a ride, or if they just felt trapped. Sometimes my own feet felt like squirrels—that's how much they wanted to skitter along sidewalks or up trees. But just in time I remembered I had zipped my lips to promise her quiet. This is called being rememberful.

I slid back down into my seat. The Cloud settled around me and crept into my nostrils.

Mrs. Rice made her way back up the aisle and called for our attention. "The bus company assures me the bus has just been cleaned, so no more complaining. You may talk, but use your inside voices," she announced. Then she sat down behind the driver with Margaret's teacher, and the bus started up. The kids around me went back to talking again, except quietly now.

And in a different language. Olive-language.

Willy and Lilly told Olive stories about being twins, in Olive-language. Maria and Rasheed invited Olive to their wedding in it. Some of the other kids from our class actually passed notes back from the front of the bus, written in it.

Right in front of me, everyone was making friends with Olive. By next week she'd be best friends with everyone in the entire third grade. Except me, because why would she want to be friends with someone who couldn't even talk her language?

Olive must have hypnotized everyone, because nobody paid any attention to me when I growled, "Stop. Talking. Olive!"

Okay, fine—maybe nobody paid any attention to me because I only growled it to myself. Still, they looked hypnotized, all right. Lilly was practically melted over the back of her seat, smiling as if just being near Olive was a magic dream come true. "Tholivis olivis solivo folivun!" she sighed.

I slumped down. It wasn't fun—it was the opposite of fun, which is boring. Luckily, I had invented a game for extra-boring times. How you play Dead-Arm is this: Pretend one of your arms is dead. You can only move it by using your other, still-alive arm, or your teeth. If you use your teeth, put your lips over them and be very gentle, like a mother cat when she lifts her kitten, because your arm is not really dead, and teeth can hurt.

Anyway, Dead-Arm makes everything you do more interesting. I lifted my right arm with my left and dropped it onto Willy's head.

"Quit it," Willy said without even turning around. "I'm trying to draw a zombie shark, and you're messing it up."

Then he turned around and gave Olive a big, bloopy smile. "I mean, I'm trying to draw a zolivombolivie sholivark," he corrected himself.

I closed my eyes and stuffed secret fistballs into my jacket pockets. And guess what I found in there? Pine needles! This is the good news about forgetting to clean out your pockets.

I pulled them out, buried my nose in them, and kept it there for mile after mile. But after a while, I smelled all the pine-scent out of them. I leaned my head way back so I could at least smell some good bus exhaust, but it wasn't much help. By the time the doors finally opened, I was practically dead from The Cloud, like the rest of the kids. We staggered out to see the first attraction.

CHAPTER

7

All I am going to say about Plymouth Rock is that
they should rename it Plymouth Pebble.

Next we got to the actual Plimoth Plantation.
We started with the Native American site. They
were planting their garden, so it smelled really good
there—like dirt that was just waking up, and things
that wanted to grow. "Corn and beans and squash,"
our guide told us. "Five seeds of each in every
mound. Five is a lucky number for Wampanoags."

For my family, too, I thought to myself, remembering the Pentagon.

Next we lined up with our partners at the gates of the Seventeenth-Century English Village. The guide reminded us that everyone inside was an actor, pretending to be a real person who was at the Plimoth Colony in 1627. "They'll be going about their everyday routines. Feel free to ask them any questions, or help with their chores."

Even though Margaret was ahead of me in line, I saw her face when the guide said that. It looked as if what Margaret had heard was, "Feel free to roll around in some garbage." She was still shuddering as we filed inside.

The first thing we passed was a pen full of pigs. Margaret had thrown her arms over her head and run down the road, but Olive and I stopped. The pigs didn't look like actors to me—they looked like real, live pigs. There were big ones, little ones, and even some baby piglets, crawling over their mother.

A Pilgrim man in red balloony pants came over and tossed a pail of scraps into the pen. The pigs got pretty excited about that, and a group of chickens came skidding over too. The way those chickens ruffled and clucked and bobbed their heads over the scraps reminded me of my grandmother and her friends gathered around the refreshment table at bingo.

I laughed about that, and one of the chickens raised its head to look. It left the flock and came over to investigate Olive and me. I had never seen a real, live chicken before, so I bent down for a good look. It was so pretty that it could have been a chicken-shaped sugar cookie—one that was all speckled with butterscotch sprinkles and had a red-frosting Mohawk on top of its head.

"Hi, chicken," I said. "Nice hat."

"That's its comb," Olive said. "*Colivomb*."

The chicken twirled around and pretended to be extremely busy studying some dirt. "Look, it's playing I Am NOT Interested in You!" I explained to Olive.

I walked over to the fence and began to admire the garden beyond it. "Pay no attention to it, and it will follow us. *She* will follow us, I mean," I corrected myself, remembering about chickens and roosters.

And sure enough, the chicken did. She walked right over my foot, as if my sneaker was just another piece of the road to her. I bent down again, and the chicken darted off, as if she had suddenly realized she was late for a really important chicken meeting.

Before I could follow, Olive took my hand and pulled me down the village road behind our chaperone. The chaperones had all stopped in front of the little Colony houses and were motioning for their groups to go inside. I looked up and down the road to wave good-bye to my chicken. I didn't see her, but halfway down, I noticed Margaret. She was standing all alone, with her head drooping and her hands in her pockets.

When Olive and I went inside, I understood: Margaret was right. "Your floor is dirt," I told the Pilgrim lady inside. Which she already knew, because she was sweeping it. "You're sweeping the dirt off *dirt!*"

The Pilgrim lady stopped sweeping and stared at her floor for a minute. She looked really disappointed at what she saw. "My husband promised me a wooden floor like we had in England," she said with a sigh. "That was seven years ago."

"Do you miss your home?" I asked, looking around the dark, smoky house. *I* sure would miss my home if I had to move here.

"Oh, no," the Pilgrim lady said. "The New

World is the place for us." Then she leaned on her broom to think about it a little more. "Well, I miss apples," she said at last. "We had all different kinds in England. Oh, I'd love to bite into a pippin right now! And how I would fancy a splash of cider with my stew . . . or beer," she said, leaning over to eye Olive and me more closely. "I don't suppose you've got any beer with you, travelers? We've run low."

I laughed at her joke. "Our parents wouldn't give us beer!"

But then I found out she wasn't joking! "What's the matter with them?" she asked. "Don't they love you? All our children drink beer."

"For real?" Olive asked.

"Of course!" the woman said. "You don't think we'd let them drink the water, do you? Look at this." She pointed to a bucket of water beside her table. "It's clear! There's nothing in it! That can't be good for a person."

"Then what's it for?" Olive asked.

The Pilgrim lady pointed to a bowl of dried peas. "Soup. They need to be washed first."

Which gave me a great idea. "Do you need any help?" I asked.

"Around here, always!" The Pilgrim lady wiped her hands on her apron and held the bowl out to me.

I took it, and picked up the bucket of water, too. Then I stuck my head out the door. "Margaret," I called down the road. "Come over here!"

Margaret walked over with her arms folded across her chest. She squint-eyed me.

"Here's a doing thing for you," I said. When I explained, Margaret brightened up. She sat down on a bench beside the house and began washing the peas, one by one, until they gleamed.

Olive and I sat down beside her, and the Pilgrim lady came out with some sewing and joined us.

I asked the Pilgrim lady if she had any tattoos, which I ask every grown-up I meet because you never can tell who's got one under their clothes. The Pilgrim lady answered no—but she'd seen a few on some sailors on the *Mayflower*.

"Why did you leave, anyway?" Margaret asked.

The Pilgrim lady told us about how it had been in England. It was the story we had learned in school—about how the king of England was bossing his people with some new church rules that they didn't like—but it sounded sadder the way she said it. "Burdensome rules," she called them. "They did not suit us. So we left."

Margaret's face sagged at that answer. I knew what it had reminded her of: the sixth graders, bossing her around with their new rules next year. I bet Margaret was thinking, *Great, so I should just find a New World to colonize.*

Luckily, the butterscotch-speckled chicken came over then and pecked at my sneaker laces, so I could change the subject.

"What's her name?" I asked the Pilgrim lady.

Secretly, I was hoping the Pilgrim lady would say she hadn't thought of a good name yet, did I have any suggestions? Then I would get to tell her a great name that I saw in the bathroom yesterday, which is where I get all my pet names. It was written on a tube of cream my mother rubbed into her belly each night so it wouldn't explode. That

Pilgrim lady and her chicken would be so happy with a beautiful name like *PreNata-Stretch*! And okay, fine—Olive would know that I was very talented at something, even if I couldn't do Olive-talk. So I asked again, "Does she have a name?"

The Pilgrim lady looked at me as if I'd just asked her if her chicken had a pair of ice skates.

"Isn't she your pet?" I asked.

"Pet?" she asked back. "Oh, we don't have the luxury of keeping pets here."

"Oh. So you just have her for giving eggs," I said. Which I thought was a little selfish. I didn't tell the Pilgrim lady that, though.

"Eggs, yes," the Pilgrim lady said. "And after that"—she pointed over her shoulder at her house—"into the stew pot."

I jumped up. "What . . . ? Into the . . . You mean . . . *eat* this chicken?"

Margaret put the bowl of peas down and stared at

me. "You sound just
like your mother,
Clementine! When
she can't finish her
sentences."

I ignored her. My heart
had started pounding
really hard, like a
fist that was so
angry it wanted to

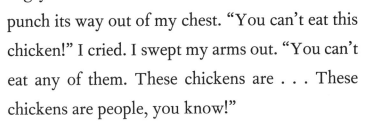

punch its way out of my chest. "You can't eat this
chicken!" I cried. I swept my arms out. "You can't
eat any of them. These chickens are . . . These
chickens are people, you know!"

The Pilgrim lady looked at me as if I had told a
joke, then she went back to her sewing.

"What do you think is in your sandwich today,
Clementine?" Margaret asked. "You eat chickens
all the time."

I looked down at PreNata-Stretch. She was stalking away from me as if she knew what Margaret had said. I hurried after her and bent down to look her in her little red chicken eye. Then I moved to her other side so I could look her in her other little red chicken eye. I wanted her to know I was serious. "Not anymore I don't," I promised her. "Not. Any. *More!*"

PreNata-Stretch cocked her head to study me; then she strutted over to join her friends. Olive came up behind me.

"This is so terrible," I said, without looking back at her, since I was trying not to cry. "Look at their faces. These chickens just want to play some chicken games and live in a nice chicken house with their families. I know it's not the Pilgrim lady's fault. She's just an actor, and she's not really going to eat them. But in real life, everyone else does. And lots of other kinds of animals, too."

"Nolivot molivee," said Olive.

I still didn't want to look at Olive, but I turned around to give her a quick side-eye. "What do you mean, not you?"

"OlivI'm oliva volivegolivetolivarolivian."

That one took me a minute. I wiped my face and turned around. "You are?"

Olive nodded. "OlivI dolivon't oliveat olivano-livimolivals."

"Oh," I said. I looked back. The chickens had stopped pecking and were staring at us. Their faces looked really worried.

"Me, too," I said to Olive. "I'm a vegetarian. I don't eat animals."

I turned back to the chickens. "I mean it," I said, with my pledge hand over my heart. "Starting right now."

* * *

The last place we visited was the *Mayflower*. It was my favorite part of the field trip, because it smelled the best on that ship—like tar and wood and salt—and there were lots of *doing* things. It also gave me the great idea of building my own boat when we went to visit my grandparents in Florida next winter. I was getting pretty good with my tools, so all I needed was some wood and some tar, and a sheet for a sail. One of the sailors told me, "Well, it's a bit more complicated than that, but you're on the right track." Then he

rolled up his sleeve to show me his tattoo.

But all the time I was having fun on the *Mayflower*, some of my Clementine sections were thinking about that chicken. And about the rest of the animals at Plimoth Plantation, and in the rest of the world.

When it was time to eat, we lined up with our partners to get our lunches from the buses, and brought them back to the picnic area. I opened my lunch box, but the sight of my chicken sandwich made we want to cry again. I snapped it shut.

Mrs. Rice caught my eye and patted the space beside her. I guess she thought I was still worried about the no-eating-sounds rules, and so she was offering to protect me from the fourth graders. Which was so nice! It made me wonder what Mrs. Rice had been like as a kid—before her feet grew up and wanted to be strapped into car seats all day. Had she had it with bossy kids and their rules too?

I started to get up to go over there, but then I realized something surprising: I didn't care about the fourth graders and their stupid rule anymore. I had used up all my caring on my chicken, and there just wasn't any left for them. So I waved at Mrs. Rice to thank her, but I shook my head no.

Beside me, Olive tapped my knee and held out her lunch box. "It's vegetarian," she said. "I'll share with you."

I saw hummus and pita chips, celery sticks, two apples, and a cookie. Even a person with cotton balls for teeth would make noise eating this lunch.

The fourth graders were going to go out of their minds when she took a bite.

Suddenly, even though my teacher was all the way on the other side of the picnic area, I imagined I heard his voice. *I know I can count on you to make Olive feel comfortable on the field trip. I know I can count on you.*

"Thanks," I said to Olive. I took a pita chip and loaded it with hummus. Then I stood up. I looked over at the harbor and imagined for a minute what those Pilgrims must have thought when they were stepping onto the *Mayflower*: *Finally, we're getting away from those stupid rules in England!*

I sure wished I could get on a boat and sail to a New World right now. I'd take Olive with me, and Margaret, and Principal Rice, and anybody else who thought the silent-eating rule didn't suit them.

Instead, I raised the pita chip to my mouth and chomped down, as loudly as I could. "Cr-*UNCH!*" I yelled, in case anyone had missed it. Then I unstuck my tongue from the hummus on the roof of my mouth with a *SNICK!* so loud it probably sent tidal waves rocking the *Mayflower* at the dock.

The whole picnic area went silent.

All one hundred kids turned to gape at me.

The fourth graders looked shocked. The third graders looked worried. Margaret pulled her jacket over her head, as if she couldn't bear to watch.

Only Olive didn't seem interested. She snapped a celery stick in half and bit down.

I grabbed a celery stick and crunched so hard the sound echoed off the buildings. Olive took a drink from her juice box. I fake-glugged from mine. Everything Olive did, I did louder.

Waylon was the first person to join me. He stood up and growled like a lion as he gnawed off

a piece of fruit leather, then smacked his lips around it.

Maria was next, and you never heard

grapes pop so loudly. Joe sloshed his soup like a cement mixer. And then, one by one,

all my friends came over and joined my team—the "Who Cares How Loud You Eat?" team.

Mrs. Rice stood up. At first I figured I was in trouble for committing the giant crime of Embarrassing Our School on the field trip. One good thing about getting in trouble in front of the principal, though—at least you can't get sent to the principal.

But you will not believe what Principal Rice did next. She looked me right in the eye and raised her hands up over her head in a thumbs-up. I knew it was a private

Good job! meant for me, but the other kids must have thought it was meant for them, too. More and more third graders joined in, snapping their jaws around their sandwiches, snicking and gulping and crunching as loudly as they could.

Pretty soon some of the fourth graders got in on it too. And then, finally, even the mean ones who had started the whole stupid no-eating-noise problem in the first place.

In the end, Olive was the only one eating her lunch like a normal person. She was probably thinking, *The kids in this new school sure are a bunch of loud eaters!* But so what? The thing that mattered was that if my teacher looked over at her, he would know he had been right to count on me. His newest student looked really comfortable.

Olive nudged my elbow, then handed me her second apple. I was just about to take a nice loud bite when I remembered something. I got up and went over to Mrs. Rice. "May I go visit the Pilgrim lady?" I asked her.

Mrs. Rice looked down the road at the village and nodded. "Take your partner with you, and come right back."

Olive and I found her, pulling weeds in her garden. She looked pretty tired, but she perked up when she saw us. "Did you find some beer after all?"

"Nope. But we brought you this." Olive and I waved good-bye and left that Pilgrim lady gazing at her apple with a *Wow! I must be dreaming* face that could probably be seen back in England.

CHAPTER
8

Back on the bus, The Cloud was thicker than ever. We sank into our seats, and the kids around me began to talk about the field trip.

In Olive-talk. Which sounded even weirder because they were holding their noses against The Cloud. I slumped against the window and watched the scenery whiz by. I learned that if I kept my eyes locked in one position, I could make the trees look like they were in a blender. Which was fun, but not fun enough.

Olive elbowed me. "Tell them about the

cholivickoliven, Clementine."

I still didn't have any caring left because of that chicken. "You do it. It will sound good in Olive talk. Which I can't do," I admitted.

Olive waved her hands like that was nothing. "Oh, me too. I had a hard time too," she said. "When I was first inventing it, my mouth got all confused. I had to go one sound at a time."

Suddenly I was reminded of what my dad had said when we were working on the Pentagon. "Say one word, really slowly, Olive. One sound at a time," I asked.

Olive held out her hand. "Huh."

"Huh," I repeated. So far so good.

"Huh. Olive," she said, stopping after each part.

"Huh. Olive," I said slowly.

"Huh, Olive, and," Olive said.

"Huh, Olive, and," I repeated. "Huh-Olive-and! Holivand! I did it!" I shook Olive's holivand.

"Th-olive-anks," I said. "Tholivanks!"

Amanda Lee's head popped in between us. "Teach me, too?" she begged Olive.

I changed seats with Amanda Lee so Olive could talk with her and I could talk with Margaret without our necks twisting off.

Except for washing the peas, I knew Margaret hadn't had a very good time on the field trip. "But hey!" I said to cheer her up. "No more eating-sounds rule!"

Margaret leaned over and picked some imaginary lint from her skirt. "I couldn't do it," she whispered. "I wanted to, but I just couldn't."

"Margaret, what makes you so afraid, anyway? What do the mean fourth graders do?"

Margaret dropped her head and whispered, "I don't know. They never said."

"What?" I yelped. Let me tell you, I wanted to say a whole lot more. I wanted to say how crazy it was. I wanted to say, *You were so afraid all this time, and you didn't even know what you were afraid of? It wasn't some kind of actual* torture? *And you made me afraid of it too?* But one look at Margaret's face made me stop talking. It made me realize something: Margaret was just afraid of breaking rules. Margaret liked rules so much she even liked the ones she didn't like.

I patted her shoulder, and Margaret let me, even though she is usually not so fond of people touching her. "Margaret," I said instead of all I wanted to say, "I'm going to be in fourth grade soon."

"Uh-huh."

"Margaret, lift your head up. Look at me."

Margaret didn't lift her head, but she side-eyed me for a second. "What?"

"I'm going to be a fourth grader in September—that's only about a hundred and fifty days away. I need to learn how to boss people," I said.

"You're so lucky," she said. "Fourth grade for a whole year."

"Except that I don't know how to do it," I said. "When I try to make Spinach do something, he falls over laughing and then he goes and does the opposite. I need to practice on someone. And you're going to be a fifth grader, so you need to practice how to be bossed. Let's try it now."

Margaret groaned, but then she surprised me. "You're right. Let's do it."

I dug around in my backpack for my dad's bag of pecans. I took out a nut. "All right, ready? Margaret, I am *ordering* you to break the no-eating-sounds rule!"

"No way," Margaret said, backing away and eyeing the pecan like it might be trying to bite *her*. "I want to, but you have to boss me better. You have to give me an or-else."

"Okay, fine," I said. "Margaret, crunch, or else!"

Margaret rolled her eyes. "Or else *what?* You can't just say 'or else'—you have to give me an or-else *thing*."

"Okay. Um . . . or else I won't give you any apples from my new tree."

"No, no, no!" Margaret shook her head so hard a barrette flew off and clattered under Maria and Rasheed's seat. "You have to make it a

really bad or-else. Something that will make me do it."

"Hmmm . . ." I looked around for inspiration. "How about . . . or else I won't climb down there and get your barrette for you. I'll make you go and get it yourself."

Margaret pasted herself against the bus seat and shuddered at the horror of what might be under there. Then she screwed her face up and thought for a minute. "These are my favorite barrettes and now I only have one and I hate only having one because . . . what side will I wear it on? But it's still not bad enough. It has to be something *really, really* bad."

"Okay, then." I revved up my bossiest face. "Margaret, I order you to break the rule and crunch that pecan, or else I *will* crawl under that seat and get your barrette and then I'll *clamp it back in your hair!*"

"*AAAAUUUURRRRGGGGHHHH!*" Margaret screamed, and threw her arms over her face. "That's horrible! That's a good one, all right!"

Then she lifted a nut and brought it to her face. She opened her mouth. She inched the nut closer. Then she curled her lips over her teeth.

"Nope," I said. "Bare teeth. Or else . . ." I jerked my thumb toward the bus floor.

Margaret took a deep breath and nodded. She opened her mouth so wide I could see all her braces. And then she bit down.

Now, compared to what I had done at lunch, Margaret's bite sounded like a moth's footstep. It sounded like a moth's footstep if the moth was crossing a carpet. And wearing socks. But I had heard it, and Margaret had heard it, and it was enough for both of us.

We sat there quietly, having a proud time for a while and trying not to breathe The Cloud.

"Wow," Margaret said after a minute. "You're good at bossing people."

Usually when someone says I'm good at something, I feel happy. But Margaret's compliment made me feel a little sad. "Thanks," I said anyway. "You were a good teacher."

"Thanks," Margaret said back. She looked a little sad about her compliment too.

Or maybe, I thought, maybe she was sad because after all that being-bossed, she still only had one barrette.

I looked down at the bus floor. Mrs. Rice was right—it did look as if it had just been cleaned.

"I'll be right back, Margaret," I said. Then I slid to the floor and twisted under the seat.

The smell from The Cloud was much worse under there. I held my breath and wriggled between Rasheed's and Maria's feet and then under the next seat, and there I found Margaret's barrette. I rolled onto my back to tuck it into my jacket pocket.

Just as I was about to crawl back, I saw something weird. On the underside of Willy and Lilly's seat, there was an arrow.

A real arrow, not a drawn one. A long, thin, black metal arrow, stuck to the bottom of the seat with a wad of chewing gum.

It looked familiar, but I couldn't place it at first.

And then I did. I saw an arrow just like it every day, on every clock inside our school!

I suddenly knew: this was the minute hand Baxter had stolen from Principal Rice's clock. It was pointing to a screw at the edge of the seat. And it was still telling the time: Baxter's stolen minute hand was telling me it was time to unscrew the seat covering.

I'd have to be like Baxter to do it, though: I'd have to use any ways and means available to achieve my goal. And right there, in my pocket, I had a perfect ways-and-means: Margaret's barrette. Its end was like a thin screwdriver blade.

I fitted it into the head of the screw. Just then, I felt a kick on the bottom of my sneaker. "What are you doing under there?" Maria's voice asked.

"Being resourceful," I answered.

Then I went to work. It was hard to see under there, and hard to work, because the screw was about an inch from my nose. It was hard to breathe, too, because the smell from The Cloud grew stronger every minute. My fingers kept slipping off the barrette, and the barrette kept slipping out of the slot, but I kept reminding myself, *One tool, one hand, one step.* And finally I got the screw out.

The seat covering flapped down a little and a strip of paper fluttered down. I picked it up. In fat-marker, loud, capital letters the note said, "I AM NOT A LIAR!"

I tugged on the seat cover, and heard something slide. I skidded away just as a sandwich bag filled with dark, slimy glop splatted to the floor.

I scrambled to my feet. "Charlie," I hollered up the aisle, "I found your Egguna sandwich!"

Rasheed jumped up as if the seat was on fire and grabbed Maria's hand. "I will rescue you!" According to Rasheed, rescuing each other is a big part of being in love with someone.

Next, Willy leaped out of his seat, and for the first time in her life, Lilly did exactly what Willy did, instead of the other way around. Pretty soon everyone on the bus knew that I had found The Cloud, and that Baxter had left it.

Mrs. Rice steamed down the aisle in her car-seat sandals, armed with a magazine and another plastic bag. She scraped up the sandwich with the magazine and knotted the plastic bag around it, and told us we could open the windows. Her face was like a billboard sign—one you could read a mile away. *I must have been crazy to go on this trip*, her face said. *I must have been crazy to want to be a principal in the first place. Get me out of here!*

Which was a lot for a face to say, even one as big as Principal Rice's.

I flopped back down next to Margaret. I could tell she was wishing there was a bathroom on the bus so she could push me into a hot shower. Instead, she ripped open a bunch of wipes.

"We'll start with the hands. One wipe for each finger." Margaret said it with a deep frown. But somehow, I thought she looked pretty happy.

My parents were on the couch, fake-wrestling Summer Squash for the TV remote, when I walked in.

My mom looked up. "How was Plimoth Plantation?"

"Good," I said. I dropped my backpack. "I met a chicken. I'm a vegetarian."

My heart started to rev up again, punching me from the inside. It hurt. A lot. "Unfair . . . If it was Moisturizer . . . Who says we should . . . Chickens don't eat *us*. . . ." My words tumbled over each other. My arms pinwheeled. My voice rose higher and higher. I couldn't stop.

"Remember how you said we're *all* us, and we're *all* them, and we're all on the same team, Mom? Well, that should mean chickens, too. The Pledge should be a promise about 'liberty and justice for all, including chickens, *which we won't eat.*' 'My Country 'Tis of Thee' should be a song about 'the home of the free, including chickens, *which we won't eat.*' And all other animals. We have to be fair!"

My brother let go of the remote and gaped, as if he'd never seen me before.

My father leaned back and scratched his head, repeating, "*Vegetarian?* As in, *No bacon?*" over and over, as if he couldn't understand such a ridiculous thought.

And through it all, my mother just sat there looking at me with her head cocked and a funny expression on her face. I recognized it—it was the look she wore whenever our baby moved inside her. She says it feels like there's a little otter in her belly, wriggling and swimming around. She always looks half baffled and half amazed at the crazy-weird miracle of that.

Except now my mother didn't have her eyes closed. She was looking right at me. Finally she spoke. "Why, Clementine," she said, with the same *What-the-heck-is-this-crazy-weird-miracle?* expression. "I think you're going crunchy on us."

My dad stopped, mid-"*No bacon?*"-ing. "You're right," he said. "Our daughter is going—"

"Hold on," I said. "You know about 'going crunchy,' Mom?"

My mother rolled her eyes. "Oh, please. Of course I know. I know everything that goes on in this family."

My dad drew a quick secret Pentagon in the air behind her and shook his head to say, *Nope, she sure does* not *know everything!*

I winked back and stretched my hands out so I could give my mom a tug-up from the couch. "So, okay? No more eating animals, right?" I asked her.

"I don't know, Clementine. It's a lot to think about," said my mom. She was wearing the crazy-weird-miracle look again. "But it doesn't matter. What matters is that you really believe in this. And tonight, that makes you the captain of this family's team."

Waylon!
One Awesome Thing

SARA PENNYPACKER

PICTURES BY
Marla Frazee